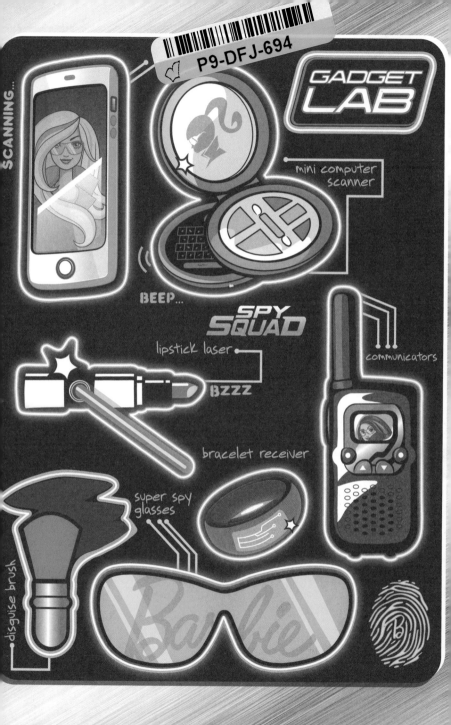

Special thanks to Venetia Davie, Ryan Ferguson, Charnita Belcher, Tanya Mann, Julia Phelps, Sharon Woloszyk, Nicole Corse, Darren Sander, Rita Lichtwardt, Debra Zakarin, Karen Painter, Stuart Smith, Carla Alford, Julia Pistor, Renata Marchand, Michelle Cogan, Shareena Carlson, Kris Fogel, Rainmaker Entertainment and Conrad Helten and Lilian Bravo

Published in the United States by Random House Children's Books, a division of Penguin Random House LLC, 1745 Broadway, New York, NY 10019, and in Canada by Random House of Canada, a division of Penguin Random House Ltd., Toronto.

Random House and the colophon are registered trademarks of Penguin Random House LLC.

ISBN 978-1-101-93143-1 (trade) — ISBN 978-1-101-93145-5 (ebook)
randomhousekids.com
Printed in the United States of America
10 9 8 7 6 5 4 3 2 1 First Edition

Adapted by Molly McGuire Woods
Based on the screenplay by Marsha Griffin
and Kacey Arnold
Illustrated by Ulkutay Design Group

Random House 🏠 New York

*B*arbie put on a sparkly pink leotard and stretched for her gymnastics meet. She and her teammates, Renee and Teresa, watched other teams practice. One team's star, Patricia, hit another perfect landing.

She's good, Barbie thought.

An announcer called: "Welcome to the Golden Cup Championship Qualifying Trials. Athletes, take your places!"

"I'm not ready," Barbie said nervously to Renee and Teresa. "I want to practice

Pandora's Pyramid one more time."

"You'll be great," Teresa said.

Barbie sighed. If only she believed that.

"Go, Renee!" came a shout from the stands. It was Renee's aunt Zoe.

Barbie, Teresa, and Renee took their places and began their routine. They flipped and cartwheeled. They tumbled across the mat. The audience cheered.

It was time for Pandora's Pyramid. To pull it off, Barbie had to land on Renee's and Teresa's shoulders. So far, she had stumbled on every landing.

Barbie took a deep breath. She tumbled

toward her teammates. Then she sprang into the air. But instead of landing on her friends' shoulders, she landed on the mat! The audience gasped.

Barbie groaned. "I totally psyched myself out," she said as the girls left the gym together.

Teresa put a hand on her shoulder. "Don't be so hard on yourself. We still qualified for the championship."

Renee's cell phone rang. She answered it on speaker, and Auntie Zoe's voice rang out. "How would my three favorite gymnasts like to join me for a picnic?"

Renee looked at her friends. They nodded. It would be good to take their minds off the competition.

"Sure, sounds fun," Renee replied. "Text me the address."

A short while later, the girls arrived in the hills of Hollywood. They were right under a sign. But where was Auntie Zoe?

"Are you sure you put in the right address?" Teresa asked.

Just then, a secret door opened in the side of the hill.

"Let's check it out," said Barbie.

Cautiously, the girls entered the hill. They found themselves in a command center. High-tech computers lined the walls. A holographic world map spun in the center of the room. Nearby, some workers tested a jetpack.

"Wow!" Teresa exclaimed.

"Hello, girls," a familiar voice greeted them. It was Auntie Zoe!

"Welcome to I3—the International Intelligence and Innovation Agency."

"*You're* the head of an international intelligence agency?" Renee asked.

Auntie Zoe nodded. "Yes, and we need your help."

Barbie was curious. How could they help a spy agency?

Auntie Zoe explained. "There have been robberies of rare gemstones recently." She showed the girls pictures of the gems on a holographic screen. "The gems themselves aren't dangerous, but if they are put together correctly, they can be. Many years ago, the agency developed a gem-powered weapon called the EMP machine. It stands for electromagnetic pulse. The machine was too dangerous, so we took it apart. But it looks like someone is trying to put it back together."

Barbie frowned. Why would anyone do that?

Auntie Zoe explained that the machine was powered by nine gemstones. Five had been stolen, the agency had one, and the other three were missing.

"We must stop the jewel thief and recover the remaining three gems," she continued. "If we don't, the thief can use them to re-create the EMP machine and use it for harm."

"Why not just get them yourselves?" Renee asked.

Auntie Zoe pulled up a video of the jewel thief. The figure was wearing all black and dressed like a ninja with cat ears.

The thief was doing a series of gymnastics moves to avoid being captured. "As you can see, the thief is very athletic," Auntie Zoe explained. "So far the thief has been uncatchable! But *you girls* could change that. You have power, strength, and focus. With more training, you could help us catch this thief!"

"We're going to be secret agents!" cried Barbie.

"I knew I could count on you," Auntie Zoe said. "Let's get you set up."

*M*oments later, the girls followed Auntie Zoe into another command center.

"When will the thief make the next move?" Barbie asked.

"Any day," Auntie Zoe replied. "We need to get you field-ready ASAP."

A man wearing a black suit marched into the room.

"This is Agent Dunbar," Auntie Zoe said. "Your training specialist."

Behind Agent Dunbar, an adorable

robotic kitten mewed. The girls squealed. They scrambled to pet the cute cat.

"What's your name?" Barbie asked, scratching the kitten under its chin.

"Violet," the kitten replied.

"Did that kitten just talk?" cried Teresa.

Auntie Zoe nodded. "Violet is a techbot. We use them for field surveillance."

"Ladies, it's time for a tour," said Agent Dunbar.

First, they visited the disguise closet. It was full of hats, wigs, and costumes for undercover agents.

Next, they stopped at the invention lab. "Every gadget and weapon used in the field is created and tested here," Agent Dunbar explained. "Our resident inventor, Lazslo, is the best in the business."

"Welcome!" Lazslo said. He handed Teresa a techbot that looked like a dog.

"This is your techbot. His name is Percy!"

"Who's a handsome boy!" Barbie cooed.

Percy spoke in a gruff British accent. "I *know.* I'm *adorable.* Let's lose the baby talk, okay?"

Barbie laughed.

"What's this?" Renee picked up a purse from a nearby table. Suddenly, a wire shot across the room from inside the purse. "Rappelling purse—awesome!" With the touch of a button, Renee could scale down the side of any building!

"All right, playtime is over," Agent Dunbar announced. He turned to Lazslo. "*If* they make it past training, I'll bring them back for the rest."

Barbie bit her lip. *If?*

*B*arbie and her friends zipped into ninja suits and snapped on utility belts. They clipped smart watches onto their wrists. Agent Dunbar nodded his approval.

Suddenly, Barbie disappeared!

Agent Dunbar sighed. "I forgot to tell you—there's a button on your belts that activates stealth mode."

"Cool!" Renee and Teresa cried, quickly disappearing like Barbie.

For the rest of the day, Barbie, Renee,

and Teresa trained. They scaled walls with their rappelling purses. They dodged zigzagging laser beams in a maze. They practiced communication with Percy, who would be with them on all their missions.

They even completed an elevated obstacle course that was filled with green-eyed robots. Working together, the girls reached the finish line quickly!

Agent Dunbar shook Barbie's hand. "Congratulations," he said. "You are cleared for your first mission. Go get your gear."

In Lazslo's lab, the girls chose their gear. Renee picked a makeup compact–heat scanner. The scanner would help them detect heat coming from laser alarm systems or other bodies in a dark room. Teresa grabbed fake nails that acted as an air keypad. All she had to do was tap the air and a holographic keyboard and screen appeared. She could have a computer anywhere, anytime! Barbie decided on a Gymnastic Launching Innovative Spy Stick, or G.L.I.S.S. It emitted beams of light and turned into a pole for vaulting and scaling walls.

The friends grinned. They felt proud to have completed their training.

As the girls exited headquarters, they heard a loud roar behind them. They turned to see Lazslo pull up in a pink motorcycle with Percy in the sidecar. Shimmering smoke billowed behind them.

"Every great agent needs a sweet ride," Lazslo said. He used a remote to drive two other motorcycles up for Renee and Teresa.

The girls high-fived Lazslo and then hopped on their bikes. Being secret agents was even cooler than they had imagined!

*T*he next morning at gymnastics practice, Barbie yawned. Secret agent training was exhausting!

Just then, her smart watch buzzed.

"It's go time," Auntie Zoe said.

"Copy that," Barbie responded. "Spy Squad en route." She and her friends ran to their motorcycles.

"Satellite has just detected a security breach inside the penthouse of billionaire Griffin Pitts," Auntie Zoe's voice continued.

Teresa used her keyboard nails to pull up a map.

"What makes you think our jewel thief is behind the break-in?" Barbie asked.

"Mr. Pitts is one of the world's biggest collectors of gems," Auntie Zoe replied. "Percy will meet you there."

Barbie signed off. She was ready for their mission to begin!

Moments later, Barbie and her friends pulled up to a sleek glass building. They hid their bikes in stealth mode.

Then they met Percy and rode the

elevator to the top floor. The loft was airy, with high ceilings. Modern glass staircases led to three levels.

"No signs of forced entry," Barbie observed.

Renee used her compact heat scanner to check for alarms. It revealed a web of laser beams. The girls would have to get through them without triggering the alarm. It would take a lot of skill and focus.

Just then, the thief peered over the second-floor balcony. "I'm up here," a voice called.

"Percy, see if you can deactivate the lasers," said Barbie. "We'll take care of this thief."

The girls ducked and leaped through the laser maze. Using the G.L.I.S.S., Barbie vaulted to the second floor.

"If that's as fast as you can go, you might as well give up now!" said the thief.

Barbie rushed ahead, almost tripping a laser beam.

"Lasers deactivated!" Percy called.

That was close, thought Barbie.

The trio chased the thief up to the third-floor staircase. Auntie Zoe wasn't kidding—this thief was athletic! Barbie surged ahead, pushing herself. "You're mine now!" she called.

The thief scaled the stairs. But when Barbie reached the third floor, the thief had vanished. Barbie spun around. Where did the thief go? Then a movement caught her eye. She peered out a nearby window. The thief was climbing down the side of the skyscraper! The girls broke out their rappelling purses. They had to follow.

They worked their way down the side of the building—until Teresa froze with fear.

"Trouble in paradise?" the thief called from below.

Barbie looked at Teresa. She was

terrified! If Barbie stopped to help her, the thief would escape. Barbie didn't hesitate. She worked her way back toward her friend. "You can do it, T," she coached.

Slowly, Teresa began to move again. Together, the friends made their way down the building. But there was no sign of the thief.

Barbie sighed. They had failed their first mission. But at least they hadn't failed each other.

Back at the agency, Barbie explained what had happened.

"Let's just chalk it up to rookie jitters and move on," Auntie Zoe declared. "Tomorrow night, the National Museum is holding a gala for its ancient gemstone exhibit."

Teresa brought up the exhibit details with her keyboard nails. "Our thief is almost guaranteed to be there," she confirmed.

Auntie Zoe nodded. "You will need to sneak into the event undercover. You are dismissed."

Barbie took a deep breath. They had a second chance. She needed to clear her head. She went to the training room to practice.

Barbie took out the G.L.I.S.S. and got to work. With the stick, she flipped faster and vaulted higher. *If only I'd had this stick at trials,* Barbie thought. *I could have landed Pandora's Pyramid!*

"You're getting good with that," Auntie Zoe said, entering the room.

Barbie's cheeks reddened. "I'm just playing around."

"You can control your mind like you control that stick, you know," Auntie Zoe said to Barbie. "Before you do whatever you are trying to do, *picture* yourself accomplishing it. *See it, then be it.*"

It sounded so easy. Could it really work? Barbie wasn't sure. But she knew one thing for certain: during tomorrow's mission, they were going to need all the help they could get.

*T*he next night, Barbie, Renee, Teresa, and Percy arrived at the National Museum's gala. They slipped through a side entrance.

"I'll radio you when I'm in position," Percy said. He disappeared down a dark hallway.

The girls entered the exhibit hall. They hid behind a large column. They touched a button on their utility belts. Their outfits changed into glittering ball gowns and matching tiaras.

The girls walked around the party. It was their best chance to get a look at the rare gems on display. They needed to see if any were missing.

Suddenly, Barbie's smart watch buzzed.

"We have a breach!" Percy called. "Northwest corner!"

Renee put on a pair of tech glasses. A map of the museum appeared before her eyes. "This way!" she motioned.

The girls raced up a spiral staircase. They entered a gallery. It was too dark and too quiet.

Renee tapped her tech glasses. "Looks like the security system has been hacked!"

Barbie scowled. "This breach was a false alarm. It was a trick to draw us away from the gems!" she exclaimed.

The girls sprinted back toward the exhibit hall. It was empty!

"Run a thermal scan," Barbie said to

Renee. "See if we're really alone."

Renee flipped open her compact. She scanned the room. A blob of red appeared on the screen. "We've got company," she announced.

A figure jumped out of the shadows. It was the thief!

"The gem!" Barbie pointed at a shiny stone in the thief's hand.

The thief leaped onto a giant sculpture and began to climb. Then the thief twisted in midair, catching a side of the sculpture near the top.

The girls' mouths dropped open.

"Impossible! That was a *triple* Arabian twist," Barbie said.

"Don't forget what happened last time you tried to keep up with me!" the thief teased.

Barbie paused. The thief was right—things hadn't gone their way last time.

What if they couldn't catch the thief this time either? It would be like failing at Pandora's Pyramid all over again! By the time Barbie pulled herself together, the thief had disappeared.

"We lost the thief," Percy confirmed.

"Again," Barbie moaned. Two failed missions. Would they even get a third chance?

The girls joined Auntie Zoe and Agent Dunbar at the agency.

Auntie Zoe shared some bad news. "The gem we had in evidence is missing."

"Unfortunately, you girls won't be the ones to retrieve it," Agent Dunbar announced.

Auntie Zoe nodded. "It's true. The director has ended your training. The stakes are too high. If the thief gets the last gem before us, all the pieces needed to revive the EMP machine will be in the thief's possession. We can't risk it."

Barbie felt miserable. If she'd only had the confidence to get the job done, they would be celebrating right now—instead of being fired.

The girls made their way to the exit.

Lazslo trailed behind them.

"I'm not supposed to do this," Lazslo said. "But why don't you keep your gear for one more day."

"Really?" Barbie cried. For the first time all day, she smiled. At least she could hang on to the G.L.I.S.S. for a while longer . . . even if she wouldn't get to use it for anything important.

The next morning, Barbie and her friends arrived at the gym for the finals. They needed to focus, but Barbie was worried.

"What if I can't pull off Pandora's Pyramid?" she asked. "I don't want to let you guys down again."

"Even if we lose, we're in this together," Renee replied.

Barbie smiled. She felt lucky to have such supportive teammates.

Then Barbie noticed superstar Patricia

working on a complicated twist. *Wait a minute,* she thought. *Was that a triple Arabian twist?*

Patricia glanced at Barbie. "I don't know why you try to keep up with me!" she gloated.

Barbie had heard those words before. Suddenly, it clicked: Patricia was the thief! "At first I didn't recognize you without your cat suit and stolen gems," Barbie said, inching closer.

"Yup, you found me," Patricia replied. "But finding and catching aren't the same thing." She brushed past Barbie and ran toward the exit of the gymnasium.

"Patricia is the thief!" Barbie called to her friends. "Let's go!"

"Wait," Teresa said. "We aren't secret agents anymore."

"This is about doing the right thing," Barbie insisted. "Isn't that why we became agents in the first place?"

Her friends nodded. The finals would have to wait.

The girls raced out the door. They jumped on their motorcycles. They could see Patricia up ahead, weaving her own motorcycle through traffic.

Suddenly, Patricia made a sharp turn. The girls were forced to slam on their brakes.

"We lost her again!" Teresa cried.

"No, we didn't," Barbie said. "I put a tracking device on her." She showed the girls a blinking red dot on the G.L.I.S.S.

screen. It was marking Patricia's path!

"Nice!" Renee exclaimed. She looked more closely at the screen. "Wait, why would Patricia be going to headquarters?"

Barbie revved her engine. "Only one way to find out!"

*B*arbie and her friends screeched to a stop in front of the Hollywood hills. They hurried after Patricia as she slipped through the secret door.

The girls snuck down the hall. They hid in the invention room and waited.

Patricia was talking to someone as she entered the room. Agent Dunbar? Robot bodyguards walked behind them.

"I just figured that if they know about me, you're next," Patricia said to Dunbar.

Barbie clapped a hand over her mouth. Dunbar was one of the bad guys! He and Patricia had been working together the whole time!

Just then, Teresa's phone rang. Dunbar's robots quickly found the girls' hiding place and captured them.

Barbie struggled to free herself. "Patricia," she pleaded. "There's still time to change teams."

Patricia rolled her eyes. "I'm not really into the whole team thing."

"But you're such a good gymnast. I looked up to you. Why would you side with him?" Barbie asked. Then she looked at Dunbar. "What did the agency ever do to you?"

Dunbar sneered, "They overlooked me for your precious Auntie Zoe."

Renee put the pieces together. "So you stole the plans to the EMP machine and had Patricia steal the gems to power it!"

Agent Dunbar slowly clapped his hands. "You are smarter than I thought. After I use the EMP weapon to cripple the agency, I can go global. Who needs to run an agency when you can rule the world?"

Patricia looked scared. "I—I just wanted to make some extra cash," she stammered. "I'm not really into world domination." She lunged for the door.

Dunbar grabbed a briefcase and fled down the hall.

Barbie fought her way free. She had to stop Dunbar! "Reprogram the robots," she instructed her friends. "I've got Dunbar."

Barbie found Dunbar and more of his robots in the command center. He opened his briefcase to reveal the EMP machine. Eight gems were already in their slots. Dunbar held the ninth gem in his hand. He popped it in place.

"You'll never get away with this!" said Barbie.

Dunbar laughed. "I already have."

Then Barbie heard a familiar voice. "Not so fast," Patricia said. "Being part of a team might not be so bad." Together, she and Barbie attacked the robots.

Auntie Zoe ran into the room. "Not on my watch, Dunbar!" She kicked a robot. It crashed into the others. They fell in a heap.

The EMP machine started to glow. . . .

"We have to contain the machine before it emits a pulse!" Auntie Zoe cried.

Barbie focused on Dunbar and the machine. *See it, then be it.* She planted the G.L.I.S.S. and vaulted through the air. She landed next to the machine. *Yes!* She shoved Dunbar aside.

Next, Renee, Teresa, Percy, Violet, and Lazslo rushed in with the rest of the robots. They had reprogrammed them to work against Dunbar.

Dunbar put his hands up. "You're supposed to be on my team!" he cried to the robots.

Auntie Zoe smiled. "Looks like you chose the wrong team."

The EMP machine started to buzz. . . .

"The machine is jamming up the signals!" Teresa cried. Their gadgets went dead. Even Percy and Violet stopped working.

"If we can detach one of the gems, we can stop it!" Barbie yelled. Renee and Teresa gave her a boost. Barbie wedged the G.L.I.S.S. under a gem, prying it loose.

It fell to the floor. The machine powered down.

The girls cheered. Percy and Violet returned to life. Barbie high-fived Patricia as the robots dragged Dunbar to the holding room.

Suddenly, Renee's smart watch buzzed. "Guys, it's time," she said.

"All right," Auntie Zoe said. "But when you're done, I want to talk about you girls coming back to the agency!"

Barbie smiled. "We'll think about it!"

"Welcome to the Championships!" an announcer called.

Barbie, Renee, and Teresa burst through the gym doors. All around them, the stands were packed with people. Lights flashed as the competition began.

Barbie hugged her friends. "Whatever happens today," she said, "I've already won with you as my team."

"Athletes, take your places!" the announcer called.

The girls ran onto the floor. As the music swelled, they worked their way through their routine. So far, so good!

Then it was time for Pandora's Pyramid. Barbie imagined herself spinning and sticking her landing. *See it, then be it.*

At the music's cue, she ran and leaped into the air. She felt herself twist. She felt herself tuck. Then she felt herself land firmly on her teammates, who were there to support her. She threw her hands proudly in the air. She'd nailed it!

The crowd went wild. Auntie Zoe caught Barbie's eye and winked.

Barbie beamed. She had practiced so hard for this moment. It felt even better than she had imagined. Now she knew that whatever challenge came her way, she had the confidence to handle it. A jewel thief, a few secret agents, and one amazing adventure had taught her that.

She looked at Renee and Teresa, and her heart swelled. Through her friends, she had learned the true meaning of teamwork. It was about believing in yourself—and in the people close to you. They were more priceless than any gem.

GADGET LAB

SCANNING...

mini computer
scanner

BEEP...

SPY SQUAD

lipstick laser

BZZZ

communicator

bracelet receiver

super spy
glasses

disguise brush

Barbie